SUPERHERO IN DISGUISE

AN ADVENTURES OF LEWIS AND CLARKE SHORT STORY

KITTY BUCHOLTZ

Daydreamer
Entertainment

Superhero in Disguise

Published by Daydreamer Entertainment

Copyright © 2013 Kathleen Bucholtz

ISBN: 978-1-937719-09-8
ISBN: 978-1-937719-08-1 (ebook)

Cover design: Stephanie Shackelford at SaRose Design
Cover images from DepositPhotos.com: Romantic couple © illustrart; Superhero cape © kimiko16; Halloween night background © igormishchenko; Purse snatcher © ronjoe; Halloween icons © angelp

Edited by Sarah Dawson

For John,
Our meeting wasn't this cute, but our happily ever after is even
better than the most blissful of fictional characters.
How lucky are we?!

SUPERHERO IN DISGUISE

Kitty Bucholtz

SUPERHERO IN DISGUISE

Finally, *a place where I can be myself. No more hiding.*
Tori Lewis grinned as she and her sister Lexie
dropped Tori's mattress on the floor. She put her hands
on her hips and caught her breath. For only a double size
mattress, that sucker was heavy. Especially when they got it
stuck in the doorway of her new house.

A place all her own, even if it was only studio sized. There
was a time Tori would never have believed she'd have her own
home. When she'd moved in with Lexie three years ago, she
was sure that was how her life would end—two old women
bickering good-naturedly with each other in between visits from
the nephew/son who adored them, no other men in sight.

Yet here she was, totally psyched about her new digs. The
first time she'd seen the place, the *Hallelujah Chorus* had
sounded in her head. It was a tiny little building in the backyard
of another house, a few blocks deeper into a not-so-great area of
the city than where she and Lexie lived now. Peach stucco with
white trim on the outside, peach and white paint on the inside, it
was totally cute without being girly-girl. The main house, a
three-bedroom ranch, sat at the front on the street, and another
little one-bedroom house leaned up against the alley.

Now Tori had her own bathroom, two—count them, *two*—parking spaces in the trash-filled alley, and a little patch of actual green grass. Well, browning grass. Halloween in Northern Michigan, and no snow in the forecast. *Awesome*.

Tori glanced out the rear window at the empty lot next door. Weeds the size of small trees and a dozen feral cats added a bit of Halloween spookiness even though it was still daytime.

A shiver tingled down her spine. Was she really going through with her plan, Operation Freedom? Or was she just pretending?

But a look through her front window showed a well-kept, if tiny, lawn with struggling rosebushes lining the sidewalk. The rosebushes were the reason Tori had signed the lease. If they could survive and thrive, so could she, right? Okay, so maybe they weren't *thriving*. They just needed some tender loving care. She would nurture the roses, and somehow they would help her grow stronger, too. She'd just have to mimic the front yard of her new home, not the backyard.

Tori sighed happily. She used one foot to maneuver the mattress up against the rear wall between two windows. "Well, the bedroom's all set up. Let's get started on the living room and office."

Lexie laughed with her and took in the entire house in one not-so-long glance. "A three-hundred-square-foot room, huh? It's not much."

"Three hundred and forty-three," Tori corrected. "And it's all mine." She threw her arm around Lexie. "For the first time in twenty-seven years, I don't have to share a bathroom. I don't even have to worry about the neighbors hearing the TV through the walls. It's a little *house*, not an apartment, and it's all mine!"

Tori squeezed her sister's shoulders to keep from clapping her hands. But the excitement came out through her feet, and she bounced on her toes. Her face was going to hurt if she didn't stop grinning. Her plan was a good one.

"Well, if this is what you want," Lexie said with a shrug, "I'm not going to rain on your parade."

But Tori could feel her sister's disappointment. It gathered and ebbed in the air as Lexie tried to hold it in. It was a weird Lexie-thing that no one could explain. Whenever she suffered a strong emotion, it radiated out. People nearby would begin to feel what Lexie felt, sometimes to a debilitating degree. It frightened their mother, Dixie. Their stepdad (who was really just "Dad") and younger siblings seemed more curious than frightened, but Dixie wouldn't allow anyone to talk about it. It was one of the elephants in the room at the family zoo.

Tori had learned to push back against the overpowering billows of Lexie's emotions, and she did so now. Pretending her sister's feelings were behind a movable glass wall, Tori focused on pushing the wall away, giving herself some emotional space. Lexie's disappointment eased back, and Tori's excitement returned.

She gave her sister another squeeze and kissed her cheek. Lexie could feel what Tori was feeling, too; that was the counterbalance. Tori focused her enthusiasm until Lexie gave in. A warmer sensation flowed between them, and Tori felt her sister relax. Much as their parents loved them, both girls had always known there was only one person they could count on: each other. Tori was determined never to let her sister down.

She grabbed Lexie's hand and dragged her back to the rented U-Haul in the alley. Today was the most exciting day of her life, and nothing was going to ruin it. One item at a time, they unloaded Tori's life. First came the computer desk Tori had bought at IKEA when she graduated from college and got her first "real" paycheck. Then came two bookcases, a TV stand, and an office chair—IKEA, IKEA, Office Max—and the little studio was already crowded.

"Are you sure about this?" Lexie asked, permanent worry lines etched across her forehead. "We haven't even brought in any boxes yet."

Tori pushed against Lexie's anxiety. Her own fear could wait until the dark night brought strange noises. She tried not to think about how creepy it might be to sleep here alone for the first time on Halloween night. "I'll have my own bathroom," Tori reminded her. "No plastic potty, no Elmo bath toys. I can light candles and take a bath for more than ten minutes."

Lexie laughed. "Okay, okay, I get it. It's paradise." She started out the door, then paused and asked, "Can I take a bath here?"

Tori chuckled as she pushed her sister through the doorway. "I'll give you a key." She couldn't remember ever feeling so good. Would she feel even better when she stole back other freedoms? Imagine—no more shrink, no more medications, no more thinking of herself as broken and in need of fixing. She couldn't quite wrap her head around what that might be like.

For twenty-two years, Dr. Huntington had been an unwanted authority figure in her life. Weekly visits and innumerable pills hadn't given Dixie the "normal" daughter she wanted, nor Tori the reassurance of unconditional love from her mother. An incident at this year's annual Labor Day family reunion had pushed Tori for the last time, and she'd begun changing her life in secret.

As she climbed up and down the three steps to her front door, bringing in box after box from the truck, Tori's insecurities rose and fell. Was this move a bad idea? She and Lexie had been doing so well living together. Lexie hadn't reverted to any of her old patterns, even early on when they were stressed about paying the rent and buying groceries. What if things took a turn for the worse and Lexie ended up back on the street, this time with her two-year-old son Ben? What would happen when Dixie found out Tori decided to stop going to the shrink? Would Tori's choices help her grow as a person or drive a wedge between her and the people she loved?

The way she went from acting strong and courageous to

scared witless and back again, maybe she *should* continue with counseling. Maybe she should've waited until Ben was in school before she moved out. That way—

"Stop!" Lexie came up behind Tori, her arms full of boxes. She dropped them against a wall and turned to Tori with that "mother" look she'd almost mastered. "Stop worrying! What's the worst thing that can happen? You move in with me again." She studied Tori's face for a moment. "And if you're worried about what Mom thinks, just…" Her voice softened. "Just stop. You're a grown woman, you need to make your own decisions."

Tori sighed and opened a box. Their dad, Danny, assured them that everything Dixie did or said was because she loved them. But a great divide existed between mother and daughters. Tori wondered if their half-brother and -sister, Kevin and Samantha, ever had to be reassured of their mother's love. Dixie doted on her two younger children.

"I don't want to make the wrong choice," she said as she put books on a bookshelf.

"Well, get over it." Lexie put Tori's little TV on the TV stand and plugged it in. "Life is full of wrong choices. Look at me. But then there are the unexpected blessings, like Ben, so… I'm not convinced wrong choices always turn out so bad."

Lexie didn't talk about "blessings" much, but when she did, her son was usually the focus of the discussion. Tori didn't know if Lexie still believed in God, but she'd changed a lot since Ben came along. Maybe if moving out wasn't the best choice for Tori, it would still turn out okay in the end.

Tori hesitated, afraid to tell her sister about her other plans.

As usual, Lexie picked up on her emotional vibe. "You're trying to decide if something else is the wrong choice?" Lexie stacked DVDs on the shelf under the TV. "You're still taking your medication, right?"

This was the reason people often thought Lexie was a mind reader. She wasn't, but she was scary good at guessing what was going on in your head based on your emotions. Tori wanted to answer the question, "Of course!" But lying didn't work very well around Lexie unless you were *very* good at it. The silence was deafening.

Lexie turned toward her, crossing her arms in big-sister mode. "You're kidding me." She sighed. "Tori..."

"I'm mostly still taking them, but I don't think I need them," Tori burst out. "No one makes *you* take any pills!"

Lexie snorted. "No one *can* make me, that's why."

Tori threw her arms wide. "But I don't have impulse control issues or an anger management problem. I'm fine!"

They stared at each other, feeling the swirl of each other's emotions, pushing and pulling in a wordless argument.

Lexie gave in first. "Fine. You decide what you think is best." She pointed a finger at Tori. "But if anything happens—"

"Like *what*? What's going to happen? No one will ever answer that question!" Years of frustration spilled out. "*Just tell me!*"

Tori watched as Lexie's face crumpled. She seemed to be trying to speak, or not to speak, Tori couldn't tell. She rushed the few feet to her sister and grabbed her shoulders. "Are you okay?"

The emotions in the room swirled with helplessness and secret fears and...was that resignation emanating from her sister? Lexie relaxed with visible effort. Her clenched jaw loosened, and her facial muscles smoothed. She took a breath.

"Remember when you were little, and you had problems at school?"

Sort of. Tori remembered the kids didn't like her. She nodded.

"Do you remember why?"

Tori thought back. "I wanted to play with them, and they wouldn't let me." The memory still hurt.

Her sister shook her head. "No, you *forced* them to play with you. That's what they didn't like."

Tori sifted through memories and old hurts. "I didn't..." She was going to say, *I didn't force them*. But then she remembered being very little, in a store, wanting a toy, and throwing a temper tantrum until her mother bought her the toy...and she remembered Dixie's face.

Her mother was afraid of her.

By the time they finished unpacking and returned the truck, dusk had settled. They picked up Chinese take-out and went to Lexie's to get dressed and hand out candy. Tori loved her Pirate Wench costume. It was sassy and bold and completely unlike her. She'd rented a blonde wig, bought some fishnet stockings, and borrowed a pair of ridiculously high heels she could barely walk in. It was perfect.

Lexie wore an adorable Little Red Riding Hood costume she'd made, and little Ben spent a couple of hours as a cute pumpkin until he screamed to get out of the puffy gourd. Immediately upon his release, he reverted to his usual angelic self.

"Just because you can't talk much doesn't mean you don't know exactly what you're doing," Tori chided him with a mock frown. He grinned at her.

Around 9:30, Tori decided to call it a night. Seeing all the costumes was fun, but tonight she was eager to go home. Besides, she needed to get away from all the little packages of M&M's. Plain, peanut, peanut butter, and pretzel—Tori loved them all. She couldn't decide if they were her kryptonite or her energy source, but she'd eaten at least six packets tonight, probably more. She tried not to let the words "stress eating" settle in her mind. Besides, the half gallon of fresh apple cider counted as a fruit. Several times over.

Lexie had been great about not pressing her to talk, but the

swirl of emotions in their apartment—that is, *Lexie's* apartment
—was cloying. Or maybe it was just the swirl of Tori's own
emotions. In any case, she wanted to get away. She needed to be
able to think someplace where no one could "hear" her
thoughts.

"Before you go," Lexie said, and pulled a box out of Red
Riding Hood's basket. She handed it to Tori.

Tori blinked at her in surprise, feeling Lexie's delight before
she even got the box open. Inside was a keychain with a tiny
silver house on the end. She gasped with pleasure and plucked it
from the box, dangling it up close for a better look. Everything
that makes up sisterly love coalesced into a warm cloud around
them as Tori hugged Lexie tight.

"Congratulations," Lexie whispered. "You're going to do
great." Her voice cracked at the end.

"Lex," Tori began. If Lexie cried, she'd cry, too.

"Go on now," Lexie pushed her away. "I know it's only a
few blocks, but call me when you get home."

Tori smiled. Home. She had her own place to live, and that
was exciting. But home is wherever you're loved, that she
knew. She squeezed her sister's hand. Sometimes blessings
were so obvious. "See you tomorrow."

As she walked home, Tori fished her house key out of her
purse and put it on her new key ring. She held it up in the
mostly dark and watched it swing. She *wouldn't* be nervous.
This was an exciting time. Nothing to be afraid of. Living alone
only meant no bathroom schedule and eating whatever you
wanted.

She tucked the key into her purse and stumbled a bit. Darn,
she'd forgotten to change back into her own shoes. She'd been
so eager to leave before the two of them burst into girlish sobs.
Oh well. It wasn't that far.

Two ghosts and a ghoul passed her on the sidewalk. A
miniature princess dressed in pink satin and lace flashed her a
toothless smile. Tori wondered why so many children were still

out trick-or-treating, and without their parents. Or their coats. The autumn night had gotten quite cold.

Teen boys dressed as the Angel of Death and the Devil leered at her cleavage as they sauntered by. Tori grimaced and pulled her lightweight jacket closer. *Teenagers.*

As she fumbled with the buttons, the Devil stole her purse.

Honestly, she should have seen it coming. The teenage boys in their hand-me-down, seen-better-days Halloween costumes exuded rebellion like it was cheap cologne. Tori stared for a second in surprise.

Tall and gangly in a red mask and black cape, the Devil took off at a dead run. Losing what little cash she had wasn't what made Tori mad. It was losing the keys to her brand-new home — and the key ring with the little silver house on it! Her first housewarming gift!

Without another thought, she gave a shout and took off after the thief. As soon as Tori began to run, she saw how *this* would end. The girl always picked last in gym class, the one who quit the track team after one day (she'd tripped over the hurdles setting them up), the girl whose greatest aerobic activity was bathing an active toddler—that girl was now running down a broken sidewalk in four-inch heels and the world's tiniest Pirate Wench costume.

A flash of red cape turned the corner ahead. So few streetlights worked in this neighborhood, the kids would get away for the simple lack of her being able to see them. Her chest tightened. She needed to *do* something.

"Drop my purse, you jerk!" she screamed with all her breath, which, granted, wasn't a lot at that point.

The tiny pirate's bodice wasn't made for sprinting, and the material lost its hold on her right breast. A swift downward glance showed an expanse of pearly whiteness bobbing up and down *and* a tree root growing up through the sidewalk. She reached up to cover her boobs at the same time that her left foot missed its jump over the tree root.

The four-inch heel went flying. Her ankle twisted under her. Tori flailed for balance with her left arm and fell, hitting the sidewalk hard. Her left leg made contact from hip to knee, shredding both skin and fishnet stockings. Both palms skidded across the concrete. Tori felt the sharp sting of skin peeling away and gasped. She landed with a thump on her left hip and bottom, the tulle petticoat under her tiny pirate's skirt flying up.

For a stunned moment, she remained in that undignified heap. Her mind created a mini-movie of what she must've looked like. A quick embarrassed laugh burst from her throat. She winced as she peeled her hands away from the sidewalk. This one needed to be entered in the Falling Hall of Fame. Then, realizing her skirt was no longer covering her lacy underwear, she slammed it down over her thighs, grimacing at the sting in her palms. No need to give the staring trick-or-treaters more of a show than necessary.

She looked toward the street corner where the Devil had disappeared. "Happy Halloween," she muttered.

JOE CLARKE SUPPRESSED THE TEMPTATION TO WHISTLE WHILE HE worked. He loved his job as a superhero, even with the long hours and the often negative press, but it didn't seem like work on Halloween. He got to dress up as anything he wanted and wander the streets looking for bad guys. Or more accurately, teenagers behaving badly.

Maybe the city's real villains were at home handing out candy with their villain-in-training children; Joe didn't know. But most of Double Bay's superheroes spent these couple of nights patrolling their neighborhoods against the only immediate threat—tomorrow's citizenry.

Devil's Night, the night before Halloween, had become a free-for-all over the years. Kids had gotten it in their heads that they could do anything they wanted this one night of the year so long as they called it a prank. Even good kids succumbed to peer pressure to become petty vandals.

At one point, things had gotten so bad that chucking eggs at cars had escalated into setting the vehicles on fire. A city-wide crackdown a decade ago had brought the situation under control. Now most of the complaints were about smashed jack-o'-lanterns, stolen decorations, trees and shrubs wrapped in toilet paper, and thrown eggs and rotten vegetables.

Last night, Joe had arrived too late to keep a house from being toilet-papered—a very quiet job that he didn't hear until he was right on top of it. But he'd managed to keep a few cars from getting egged. Of course, most of the eggs had dropped on the sidewalk when he'd scared the crap out of the kids. But better there than on a car's paint job.

This year, Joe dressed as Zorro. The black costume concealed his presence and allowed him to stop more vandalism-in-progress than he'd managed last year. Fewer smashed pumpkins and stolen decorations, less graffiti. Renting the Captain America costume last year, complete with hoodie-mask and metal shield, rated high on his geek meter, but it hadn't put the fear of God into many vandals. Zorro apparently scared them more, no doubt due to the fact that his sword looked real. Joe really liked the sword.

A flock of teenage girls rushed down a driveway and turned toward Joe. Their titters upon seeing him turned to giggling cries when Joe swept off his hat and bowed as he passed. He chuckled softly.

Dry leaves crunched under his feet as he walked the dark streets. The warm scent of woodsmoke curled into the brisk night air. An occasional gust of wind coming off the bay signaled colder weather on the way. Joe almost hoped it would snow soon. He'd bought a new John Deere Snowthrower last spring at an end-of-season clearance sale, and he could hardly wait to try it out.

A woman's scream tore through the night.

Joe swiveled toward the sound and sprinted down the street. He analyzed the night as he ran. The woman didn't sound in pain, or even scared, and she hadn't screamed again. She sounded angry. Possibly a thief then, something relatively nonviolent. He hoped so. Violence against women and children unmasked darker sentiments in Joe's heart that he didn't like to acknowledge. He scanned the empty yards. The leafless branches of the trees made it easier to see, like looking through the bare arms of motionless skeletons. Nothing.

Running feet. He crossed the street to intercept the potential hoodlum. His costumed cape flew behind him. Hoodlums, plural. Two teenagers ran toward him.

"Stop!"

Joe's command caused them to stumble over each other as they changed direction. They hopped a short fence and ran through a dark yard. A dog barked and another picked up the call. One of the teens threw something behind a parked car as he ran.

Protect her.

Joe hopped the fence and paused. He blinked and shook his head.

Protect her.

The feeling overwhelmed Joe's senses like a voice that was more than audible. Team protocol called for him to nab the boys, call the police, and find whatever had been stolen, in that order. He was sure the woman's scream was more of a yell, that she wasn't hurt, but his intellect couldn't overcome the command surging through his mind. *Protect her.*

He took a moment to search near the parked car and saw something fuzzy on a thin chain. The nearest streetlight was broken, so he couldn't see well. Perhaps a woman's purse? He'd never seen anything quite like it. Tucking the chain around his belt, he hustled down the street, looking for the woman who'd been mugged.

Turning a corner, he saw someone sprawled on the sidewalk. His heart raced. As he got closer, though, his steps slowed as alarm warmed into red-blooded admiration. A blonde pirate sat in a tumble of lace, one beautiful breast in her hand.

LEXIE'S COMMENT ABOUT TORI FORCING HER SCHOOL FRIENDS to play skidded through Tori's mind. What were the chances that she'd forced the mugger to drop her purse? Probably not very great. She shook her head. Lexie was exaggerating to make a point. Sure, Tori was unnaturally good at convincing people to do things, but that didn't mean she could *force* them to do what she said.

She carefully brushed the dirt from her fingers, not letting her palms touch, and began to put herself back into her costume. Trickier than it would seem using just her fingertips. She pulled away the bodice with her right hand, then used her left to tuck her breast back inside. But the stiff lace trim pulled at a piece of raw skin and made Tori's eyes water. She snatched her hand back. Sure enough, the lace now glistened with blood.

"Cra-ap!" she muttered. Thoughts of Bactine and Fudgsicles entered Tori's mind. Dixie had always been great about fixing life's little scrapes. Her funny little saying—"Nothing broken, no one maimed"—a smile and a hug, followed with a Fudgsicle or a homemade treat; that would forever be how Tori judged life's small injuries.

It was the big things Dixie couldn't handle.

Still trying to adjust herself properly, Tori used both hands to push and prod. It shouldn't take this much work for a B cup, but her bloody hands were half useless. She heard a soft swish of fabric on fabric, then darkness blotted out the streetlight.

Tori looked up in alarm.

Zorro towered over her. From her vantage point on the

sidewalk, he looked enormous. Dressed all in black, he had tall gleaming boots, snug breeches, a billowy shirt under a flowing cape, and the perfect Zorro hat complete with a long black feather. *Gorgeous*. Tori craned her neck. He was at least as tall as her dad, and Danny stood at six feet in his socks.

The masked man looked stricken. His mouth worked soundlessly until the words finally came out. "Can I help you?"

Tori followed his gaze to see both her hands still inside her bodice. She snatched them out. The quick movement undid some of her work, so she hunched her shoulders a bit to block his line of sight, pushed and prodded—bloody hands or no—and sat up straight again.

She cleared her throat. "Thank you, no, I'm fine."

He raised his eyebrows. Even in the darkness, Tori was sure she saw him fighting back a smile. Then she realized what he meant—not her *boobs*, her *situation*!

"Oh!" She felt blood rush to her face. "I'll be fine. I just have to get my purse back." She moved to get up and winced.

Zorro bent to one knee. His cape swirled around them, giving Tori the strange feeling that they were alone together. Her heart raced. Behind the mask, his eyes looked kind but intense.

He held out a fluffy pink heart on a silver chain. "Yours?" he asked. "The kid dropped it. I guess it didn't go with his outfit." Zorro had the same expression her dad and brother got whenever they looked at her purse. Kind of like they were about to heave.

Tori gasped. Sparing a glance for the dark stranger, she unclasped the heart-shaped bag to find everything still there. The mugger must've dropped it before he could open it.

"Th-thank you," she said, fighting to keep her voice steady. A wave of emotion washed over her. Not a swirl of feelings like when she and Lexie were together. It was more specific...*safe*. Similar to when she was with her sister, but deeper somehow, more stable. She was absolutely and inexplicably safe. She stared into Zorro's eyes, trying to figure out what was happening.

If it weren't for the "no men" rule, Tori would find a way to get to know this man better. She'd never felt safer, but she'd learned her sister's lessons. And her mother's. She needed an exit strategy.

"You're smiling."

Really? So was he. Had she smiled first? If so, only because of that warm, wonderful feeling wrapping around them.

Zorro's crooked smile lifted higher on the left. It made him look young and mischievous. This guy was dangerously cute. Gorgeous she could walk away from, but cute...

Tori cleared her throat and looked away. *Get a grip.* She took a deep breath to clear her head. Oh geez, he smelled wonderful. Something she did *not* want to notice. She pulled away, her nerves tingling.

"Thank you for finding my purse," she said. She pulled her right leg under her to leverage herself up, but forgot about her skinned palms. As soon as they touched the sidewalk, she gasped and curled her wrists toward her body.

Zorro leaned over and picked up Tori's hands. Turning them palm up, he grunted. "Bet that stings."

His quiet, deep voice wrapped around her heart. His touch set her mind and body at ease. She was exactly where she was supposed to be.

Focus! She shook her head and leaned back a few inches. "Not as much as my leg," she tried to joke.

"Let me see." He laid her hands in her lap and gently prodded at her skinned-up leg. "Can you stand?"

Tending to her injuries, he was more focused on her than ever. It was disconcerting, uncomfortable, and fabulous. Tori wondered what it would be like to be the focus of his attention long-term.

"I'll be fine, thank you," she said, pushing his hands away and grimacing as her palms made contact. She should go home.

Rule #1 — If you're attracted to them, they're bad for you.

Lexie and Tori had created the rules for their protection. Whoever Zorro really was under that mask, she feared he was the kind of man who would make her forget the rules.

Gathering her legs under her with as little wincing and groaning as she could manage, Tori tried to stand without giving Zorro an eyeful of black lace underwear. Before she realized his intent, Zorro grasped Tori's ribcage and lifted her to her feet. Well, not exactly to her feet; they were dangling off the ground. He held her hundred-and-not-telling pounds off the sidewalk with ease. Too much ease. As if he were holding a teddy bear. How could he do that?

The idea of "superheroes" whizzed through her mind. But no, her parents insisted that the news stories were only publicity stunts by the city and the police department to make them look like they were tough on crime. Tori had never seen a superhero, but her experience with governmental agencies made her believe they'd say anything to look better to the public. Her parents were probably right. Zorro must be a bodybuilder or something.

"See if your ankle will hold your weight," he said, and he lowered her until her feet touched the sidewalk.

Tori put most of her weight on her good foot, the high-heeled shoe holding her four inches above her normal height of five feet seven. Her other ankle throbbed. She needed a minute to get used to the discomfort before she walked home. And it was an excuse to tilt her head back and examine her savior. Oh yeah, much taller than her dad. Gorgeous, deep-brown eyes. Tori couldn't tell if the warmth she experienced came from his hands around her waist, or something else.

The attraction intensified as they gazed into each other's eyes. She wanted more. They leaned closer. Contentment and peace stirred in her heart. He wouldn't let anything hurt her, she *knew* it. She couldn't explain it, but that didn't make it less true. The silence between them turned thick and warm. It wasn't sex on Tori's mind; it was that strange, confusing feeling of safety. Either way, it came down to the same thing—she wanted to be with him.

The thought of getting closer to the electrifying man before her filled Tori's mind until her body followed. She took a step toward him on her twisted ankle—and tripped yet again.

JOE LUNGED FOR THE WOMAN FALLING AT HIS FEET. AT FIRST, when he'd held her at arm's length, he'd focused on her features —soft lips, a slender nose, pretty eyes, and was that a velvet mole? He'd gotten distracted with her breasts...soft and plump and touchable, and pretty much falling out of her costume. She looked like the cover of a romance novel. He'd never read one, but he was pretty sure the men in those books got to touch what they were ogling.

But he felt that strange feeling inside expanding. It seemed to radiate out from his chest, similar to the way his super powers gathered just before he used them. He needed to protect this woman.

This woman.

Joe swallowed. Maybe it was something he ate, heartburn from onions. No, he'd eaten lasagna tonight. Freezer dinner. Never had heartburn from frozen lasagna.

Protect this woman.

Could it be something in his superhero blood that caused this reaction? He'd never felt anything like it before, never heard of anything like it. Wherever it came from, the feeling was powerful...and strangely peaceful. He felt stronger with her in his arms right now than he'd ever felt before. Which was ridiculous since he could stop a bullet with his bare skin, but there it was. Was there something about her that was reacting to his powers somehow?

Pirate Girl gazed up at him with a look of wonder of her face. She felt it, too.

Joe chuckled.

"What?"

He tried to hold in his laughter. "Uh...well, you look even more like a pirate now."

Pirate Girl looked down at her torn stockings, spots of blood on the white lace edging of her black satin skirt. She touched her blond wig to see if it was askew. A jaunty felt pirate's hat had been sewn onto the wig.

Joe wondered about her real hair color.

Her fingers found the eye patch still covering her forehead above her right eye. She pulled it down. "Aargh! Good thing you found the little devil before I did, or he'd be shark bait by now," she said in a ridiculous attempt at a pirate voice.

Joe laughed, and Pirate Girl laughed with him.

"I love Halloween," she said. "You can be anyone you want."

The wistful note in her voice hit Joe in the stomach. He'd never wanted to be anyone else. The Clarke family superheroes went back generations. What could be better than that?

"Who do you want to be?" he asked.

The wistfulness crept into her expression and, for a moment, Joe thought she looked sad. Then she said in a low voice, her eyes dropping to his chest, "I think maybe with you I could be...myself."

Joe's protective instincts shifted up a gear and he pulled her closer. He didn't know what to say. "So you'll be falling for me often then?"

She burst into laughter. He could swear she moved further into his embrace.

He grinned. Playing the hero had never been this much fun before. The superheroes in his family had protected Double Bay for years, and Joe took his role as a guardian of the city seriously. It could be hard, lonely work, but tonight...

Tonight, rescuing this woman gave him more than just satisfaction with his work. He loved her laugh, spontaneous, full of warmth and joy. Her smiled bewitched him. He felt as if all the problems of the world were manageable, as if he were more powerful when she smiled at him.

"You have to admit, you're having a lot of problems tonight," he said. "Should I call your keeper?" He wrapped his arms more firmly around her, and she didn't protest. He felt strong enough to stop a train.

Pirate Girl laughed again. "I really should have one."

Joe let one of his hands run slowly down her back, enjoying the feel of her relaxing in his arms. Really enjoying the feel of her breasts pressed against his chest. Wondering how long he could stretch out this rescue. An hour? All night? Every night?

"You need a job?"

Joe's hand stopped moving. Could she read his mind? The job of "keeper" or "keep her"?

"Well, I am a member of the neighborhood watch," he said. "I think I could handle it."

The mole on her cheek caught his attention as she asked, "We have a neighborhood watch?"

"We do," he said to the mole. He could tell now that it was one of those press-on velvet ones, but he liked it all the same. "Unfortunately, I'm the *only* member."

Joe raised his gaze to hers as she giggled again. She did that a lot. He didn't know what she found so amusing, but he liked it. Neither too high nor too low, it reminded him of sleigh bells. Bright, warm, festive. Perfect for this time of year.

"Oh, well," she said, heaving a sigh of mock disappointment. "I guess you better not quit then." She looked around the dilapidated neighborhood. "I think we need you here."

Joe followed the rise and fall of her breasts as she sighed. "Mmm-hmm," he said.

"Hey!" She slapped at his shoulder. "I saw that."

"Wha-at?" He grinned at her. It was hard to be serious when he felt so good. It brought out the tease in him, a skill he and his brothers had developed into an art form living with sisters. "You want help putting those back?"

She shifted in her one high-heeled shoe and pushed her body more firmly into his. Joe realized she was trying to hide her exposed flesh. Her little suede jacket wasn't helping. Women and their impractical clothes. But who was he to complain, especially now?

"Close your eyes," she ordered.

"It's hard to take you seriously when you're laughing," he said, causing her mock stern look to crumble into giggles before she attempted solemnity again.

"Close. Your. *Eyes*."

Joe obeyed. His mother had raised him with good manners, but he wanted to sneak another peek. "Can I open them yet?"

She moved around in his arms, and he loosened them to give her more room to maneuver without falling again.

"Not yet."

He heard the laughter in her voice and it swirled around in his chest, warming him from the inside out. "Now?" he asked.

"No."

More movement. He could hear material sliding around, and the sound was doing things to his insides. "Now?" he asked, bringing his lusty thoughts in line before he embarrassed himself. "Now? Now?"

"O-*kay*." She laughed and one arm slid around his neck again. "You must've been someone's little brother."

He opened his eyes and looked down. "Why do you say that?" Aw, she'd even fastened up her coat. It was one of those coats that buttoned to just over her breasts. Still a pleasant view, all creamy smooth skin.

She swatted his shoulder and gave one of those delicate female snorts, the kind that could've meant anything. "Because I have a little brother."

Joe was sure she was enjoying the evening as much as he was. Then she smiled at him again, and he wanted to climb Mount Rushmore, or fly to the moon, or just toss her into the air and spin her around until she was breathless with laughter.

He wondered if she felt the pull of attraction — or whatever it was — as acutely as he did. He thought about the word for a moment and discarded it. He'd been attracted to women before, and it was nothing like this. No, this was a different kind of connection.

Protect her.

The feeling was so compelling, it was as if he were hearing voices. He couldn't explain how or why. Looking at the girl in his arms, he didn't care what the explanation was, he was happy to do his job.

His right hand caressed Pirate Girl's cheek. She sighed and laid her head on his shoulder. He let his cheek rest against her hair for a moment, enjoying the scent of her, the feel of her. And at the same time, wanting to break away.

Joe didn't need complications right now — not blond, brunette, or red-headed. He wanted to work, and he didn't want anyone or anything to make him feel guilty about that. He didn't want to end up like his father, quitting because he had children.

Just one kiss, and then I'll walk away.

Joe leaned down and captured her cheeks in his hands, tilting her face up. Her gasp of surprise brushed against his lips as he kissed her. More surprising than his lack of impulse control was her reaction. After a moment's hesitation, Pirate Girl leaned into him, her hands on his chest, her lips moving with his.

Which only made it that much harder to stop.

Vaguely, Joe registered a dog barking a distant alarm. He ignored it and pulled Pirate Girl off the ground and up into his arms so he could kiss her more easily. Her hands wrapped around his neck, and she kissed him back with gusto.

Okay. Enough. Joe reminded himself of his duties and pulled back.

Pirate Girl blinked up at him, looking dazed. Then she smiled a dazzling smile.

Joe smiled back and gave her one last soft kiss before he lowered her to her feet. A burst of satisfaction spread through his chest.

She felt it, too.

IT WAS ONE THING TO FEEL SAFE AND PROTECTED. IT WAS something else entirely for the world to light up in brilliant colors from a kiss! Tori's perspective on the world changed. Like a crooked window made straight, now everything made sense.

That kiss… She wanted another one. The way he held her now, the way he was looking at her like he wanted to do it again, made her want more. She'd never instigated a kiss with a man in her life. But everything was changing tonight.

Rule #2—If you ignore Rule #1, phone a friend and *get out.*

Lexie had told her to call when she got safely home. Tori knew her sister would want her to call now, to *get* safely home.

But tonight she and Zorro were both costumed, disguised, hidden. Safe. This was the perfect time to act on Operation Freedom. For just one night, she could be herself with no repercussions. She could try out possibilities and see what *she* thought felt right.

Tori wobbled on one four-inch heel. She thought to take off her shoe, but she liked the idea that Zorro would catch her if she fell. Plus, her mouth was four inches closer to his. Taking a deep breath for courage, she leaned against him and slid her hands up to his neck, pulling him closer. If he resisted, she hoped the embarrassment would kill her on the spot. But his mouth came down on hers quickly and easily. Needing no more encouragement than that, Tori poured herself into the moment.

Zorro's lips moved against hers, setting off grass fires throughout her body. His hands swept hot paths up and down her back, her rib cage.

Tori imitated him, moving her lips over his, running her hands over his muscular chest and back. When his mouth opened, hers followed. When his tongue touched hers, she heard a moan escape. Nothing she'd ever experienced in her life could equal this!

She let Zorro lead, but followed his moves like a prodigy. After a moment, Tori tried a few moves of her own. His arms wrapped around her in response, pulling her against his chest and off her feet again. She heard him moan, and the sound rippled over her nerves.

Everything she felt tumbled around her brain without connection—hard, soft, warm, hot, more…

Zorro stopped kissing her. He rested his temple against hers, a ragged sigh escaping into her ear. The sound went straight through her, hitting every nerve all the way to her toes. Could she be wrong? Had he not enjoyed that as much as she had? More than anything, Tori wanted another kiss.

"What are we doing?" Zorro asked, his deep voice rumbling through his chest and into hers. His arms tightened around her.

Tori's senses heightened, waiting to see what he would do. She kept her eyes closed to enjoy this last bit of passion before it was over.

His forehead slid over hers, traced the path of his breath across her cheek, closer to her mouth, closer still, until—

The touch of his lips to hers was magic and fireworks and s'mores all rolled together. His mouth and tongue fought a give and take with hers.

Rule #3—If you ignore Rule #1 and #2, don't let them see your true self.

Screw that.

She gave herself over to him, no more thinking and imitating. Tori just let go. Her fingers spread through the curls at the base of his neck, soft and silky. One hand caressed his neck, exploring upward to his cheek, smooth and soft and hard. Cupping both his cheeks, she lifted herself up as far as she could go, pulling his head down to put the last of herself into the kiss before she pulled away.

But she didn't know that more begat more. The kiss kept pulling her higher. Out of control.

Zorro pulled away, breathing hard. Tori felt bereft for a moment until he tucked her head under his chin and held her tight.

She didn't know what was happening. It wasn't just the kissing—though that was *awesome*. No, there was something deeper going on here. She shivered and pressed closer. She didn't want to leave him. She didn't want him to leave her. She wanted—

"Have you always been trouble?" he teased.

Tori sobered a bit. He had no idea. "Since the day I was born."

Rule #4—Pretend, pretend, pretend.

She couldn't do this to him. The "no men" rule had been created to protect her and Lexie from the world. They'd created a haven for themselves and it had worked exactly as it was meant to—they were alone and safe.

But even if this man, a man whose name she didn't know, even if he really could keep her safe... Well, she couldn't protect *him*. There was something odd about her sister and her, something that scared people when they found out about it. She didn't understand it, but she and Lexie were better off alone.

He sighed. "I guess I should get you home before you freeze."

Tori hid her face and her disappointment in the folds of his cape. "Of course."

"I'll carry you. Where do you live?"

He lowered her to the ground and, with a flourish, pulled off his cape and settled it around her shoulders. Tori bit her lip to keep from crying. She loved grand, romantic gestures. This would be the last one before he said goodbye.

Zorro tied the strings of the cape around her throat and adjusted the material. Tori swallowed when his fingers brushed her skin. His eyes met hers and his fingers stilled. His thumbs trailed down her throat.

She held her breath.

How could she act wisely when she didn't know which course of action was wise and which was foolish? The rules were for her protection, but Operation Freedom was about exploring what exactly God had in mind when he made her. She needed to know who she was outside of her family, outside of her psychiatrist's office, who she was on the inside.

Lord, give me a sign!

"There's something special about you," Zorro said softly, almost as if he were talking to himself.

Tori felt herself deflate. "Different," she said sadly. "Odd."

Zorro shook his head dismissively. "No, *special*. I'm not sure why, but..."

Tori held her breath. Hope battled fear. Joy began to overtake caution.

"Maybe you'd take a chance on someone like me," he said. "Maybe you'd let me see you again."

Maybe? Did dogs bark and cats meow?

"Yes!" Joy bubbled up from her toes and escaped in a wild giggle. But Zorro didn't seem to mind. He grinned back at her and pulled her close again, right where she wanted to be.

That safe, peaceful feeling overwhelmed her senses. The connection between them strengthened. She not only felt that no harm would come to her when this man was near, but she was sure she wouldn't scare him off either.

She took a moment to think. No, she couldn't remember *ever* feeling this way before. Surely, it was a sign from God. It was all she could do not to bounce on her toes and clap her hands.

It felt like the weight of the world had been lifted from her shoulders. And not just because Zorro had lifted her off the ground again. He twirled her in a circle. Tori grinned and threw her arms around his neck.

Finally, someone I can be myself with. No more hiding.

A PEEK AT A VERY MERRY SUPERHERO WEDDING

AN ADVENTURES OF LEWIS AND CLARKE NOVELLA

Read A Very Merry Superhero Wedding *now, the next story in the timeline before book one,* Unexpected Superhero

Available now at most online retailers

Two things always surprised Joe Clarke in December: the weather, and the people of Double Bay.

Some years the snow would start falling by Halloween.

Thanksgiving would be a day to have a plan B in case you couldn't make it to Grandma's house due to blowing and drifting snow. And Christmas would be both beautiful and frustrating with every outing marred by icy roads and fresh piles of snow to clear off the car.

Other years, like this year, there were a few snow showers, but hardly any of the snow stuck to the ground. The ski slopes were covered with machine-made snow. Shopping and traveling were a breeze.

And tracking potential home invaders proved more difficult.

Ah, yes, the wonderful citizens of Double Bay constantly surprised him. The young man he tracked now — that is, that his alter ego Superhero X tracked — really put the "dumb" in dumbed down. Not only was he peeking in windows in the fading light of the afternoon rather than waiting for the full dark that would fall over the city by dinnertime, but he wasn't paying attention to the security signs.

This particular yard sported a bold red and white sign near the front door — MGV Security. The sign wasn't hidden by snow either. What, did the guy think it was a Christmas decoration? Superhero X shook his head and waited. When the young man took out a pocket knife and pried the screen off one of the windows, Superhero X moved closer and cleared his throat.

The man jumped and dropped his knife. His eyes widened as he looked up — way up — into the superhero's face. "Oh! I-I-I was just...I mean, I...I live here..."

X raised his eyebrows skeptically. "What's your address?"

"It's, uh, let me think, I just moved here and..." The man looked around the yard and at the other houses nearby, searching for a helpful clue.

Taking a long black zip tie from a pocket of his super suit, X gestured. "Hands."

The man sighed heavily and sagged against the siding.

"You're not going to call the cops, are you?" He held out his hands. "I didn't take anything."

X tied the man's hands, then pressed a button on the wrist of his suit. "Superhero X to dispatch," he said. He gave the address, dispatch assured him that a police car would be there soon, then he marched the would-be Christmas thief to the sidewalk.

Pressing another button, he winced at the time. He'd have to hurry home to change after the police picked up the wannabe burglar. His fiancée, Tori Lewis, would be waiting for him — that is, for *Joe* — to pick her up from her last day at work. He didn't live far from here since this was his regular patrol neighborhood, but he still wanted to hurry.

Superhero X kept his facial expression impassive, but on the inside he could feel a grin. In five days, on Christmas Eve, he would finally marry the girl he rescued Halloween night. He could hardly wait.

Afraid a smile would break through and spoil his stern superhero expression, he brought his mind back around to work. He pressed a different button on his wrist and recorded a message with the time, the date, and the address of the house that had been broken into. Someone at MGV Security would get the information and call the homeowner to make a report.

"Someone" who was not Joe Clarke. MGV Security was a real security firm, but it was also Joe's cover job. A cover job from which he was technically on vacation for the next two weeks. Owned and operated by Joe's friend and fellow superhero Mickey Valient, a.k.a. Tick Tock, MGV provided professional security services to all of its clients, but there were also more...*discreet*...services they provided the city.

A snowball whizzed overhead.

Superhero X turned to look down the sidewalk. Two boys around eight or ten years old stood frozen in their snow suits, mouths gaping. They'd collected what little snow was on their lawn and made a half dozen little snowballs, piled at their feet.

X smiled and gave them a little salute. They whooped and jumped up and down. X grinned. He loved his job.

A Double Bay police car pulled up to the curb. Time to finish up work for the day and hightail it over to get his girl.

Tori Lewis felt butterflies square-dancing in her stomach. In a few minutes, she'd be off work to finish planning her wedding — and then she'd be away on her *honeymoon*. It almost didn't seem real.

For the last ten years or so, she had lived a quiet, semi-solitary life. Her mother Dixie and older sister Lexie were living proof that women in her family didn't make good choices when it came to men. Dixie's marriage to Tori's biological father had ended so badly that Dixie was still angry about it nearly twenty-five years later, even though her second marriage to Danny Lewis was filled with love and respect. Lexie had finally turned her life around a few years ago and found a "good" man to share it with. Then he broke it off and left when he found out she was pregnant. With those examples always on her mind, Tori had been afraid to chance the heartbreak and disaster she was sure would accompany a profession of love.

Until now.

There was something about Joe Clarke that called to a place deep within. It was like he'd opened a tiny door inside her, and Tori was finding all kinds of treasures — a joyful hope, love without worry, a peaceful sense of relief that she could let down her guard and relax and be herself.

With Joe, she felt safe in a way she never had before. Since Danny became her dad, he'd provided a sense of security when the world tumbled crazily around her, but then Joe came along and Tori felt like everything was finally going to be all right.

No, not just all right. *Beautiful*. Her life felt beautiful all of a sudden.

She shook her head a little as she filed the last of the papers on her desk. She was being silly, all head-in-the-clouds like a Disney princess. That's apparently what love did to people.

It wasn't the drugs. A niggling doubt squirmed in her head, trying to get her attention and ruin her day. No, it wasn't only that she wasn't taking her medications anymore. She'd started Operation Freedom in September. She'd been working toward finding her real self when she met Joe just after Halloween. He seemed so strong and sure of himself, it gave her strength to push forward and make new choices.

And when he proposed on Thanksgiving Day, Tori knew the time had come for Operation Freedom's grand finale. No more Dr. Huntington and his drugs. No more kowtowing to her mother.

Yes, she'd been feeling better since she stopped taking the pills, but that couldn't account for how she felt about Joe. From the moment they met, they'd had a connection that was…well, it defied explanation. They both felt like they really *knew* each other. In sync, on the same wavelength, whatever you wanted to call it. And it seemed to grow stronger every day.

Tori let her worries fade as she shut down her computer. It was almost five o'clock. Joe would be here any minute. They had one more quiet evening together before the final rush toward Christmas Eve and their wedding. Her stomach felt the butterfly gymnastics again and she let out a soft giggle.

This was real. She and Joe loved each other with an urgency and earnestness that made people fear they were merely infatuated with each other. But she knew — they both knew — it would last. They saw the world in similar ways. They believed in the same things. They'd prayed, together and individually, about the decision to get married. Waiting would only prove to others that they were ready. And they had nothing to prove.

"Oh, Tori," one of her co-workers singsonged nearby, "Someone's here to see you."

Tori's gaze flew to the doorway. There he stood. She sucked in a breath. His wavy brown hair was mussed, giving him a little boy look. So adorable. A knit cap stuck out of the pocket of his down-filled coat, and his scarf hung a foot longer on one side. Every time she saw him, he looked taller and more muscular than before. Every time she saw him, his smile made all of her nerve endings fire. Every time she saw him, she stopped breathing for a moment.

He grinned his lop-sided grin and chuckled. He always laughed when he saw her looking at him this way. Tori giggled and sighed. She knew he loved it, though. He'd told her no one had ever looked at him like she did.

Joe walked toward her and Tori felt a kind of tunnel vision come over her whole body. Every cell focused on him. And then he kissed her, and every cell burst out with a shout of joy.

Interrupted by the sound of laughter and clapping.

"Hello, beautiful," Joe whispered in her ear before he pulled away.

Tori felt her blood make a mad dash for her face. She'd never been so public in her displays of affection before Joe walked into her life. She'd been taking down Halloween decorations outside when he wandered by on a Sunday afternoon. They'd started talking and laughing and then they went for a walk together. Before she knew it, they were sharing a pizza. Then meeting again the next night, and the next.

And now here he was, staring down at her like he'd found a treasure he couldn't believe was his to keep. Tori realized she was grinning up at him only when more laughter and ribbing caught her attention.

She stepped back and said, "Let me get my stuff and I'll be ready."

"Not so fast, lovebirds," called her boss, Faith Borden. "We need to send you off in style."

Faith pulled out a foil-covered tray and another co-worker cleared a space on a worktable. As Faith pulled off the foil, all the ladies broke into the "Happy Birthday" tune but with the words "Happy Wedding to You." On the tray were homemade Christmas cookies, each with a letter in icing spelling out "Congratulations Tori & Joe!" M&M'S candies, Tori's favorite stress reliever, decorated the tops.

Tori laughed and squeezed Joe's hand before she reached over to hug Faith and the others.

"Thank you, Faith," she said as she squeezed the woman who'd become a new friend. "This is wonderful."

"Good heavens, lady," Faith said in an undertone, "When you said he was gorgeous, I thought you were using hyperbole like every other bride. He's stunning!" She giggled.

Several similar comments followed, all in whispers hidden by the hugs. One woman offered to babysit any time Tori was out of town. Tori laughed and shook her head.

She looked over her shoulder at Joe talking to Faith. It was fun to be the envy of all the women in the room, but she didn't care much what other people thought. She knew Joe was a good man, decent and kind and hard-working and funny. He'd made her laugh more in the last seven weeks than she could remember laughing in the last couple years.

And he made her feel safe. And strong. Kind of like the Zorro character who'd helped her on Halloween after she'd been mugged. Zorro had joked about being a superhero and Tori had laughed and said, there's no such thing as superheroes, it's an anti-crime publicity stunt by the city. He'd argued with her, presumably because he was staying in character as a defender of the defenseless, and Tori had argued back. The spark she'd felt that night seemed to lose some of its fire after that.

Then she'd met Joe two days later. At first, she thought maybe he was Zorro. But when she asked him, he laughed and said he was just an ordinary, everyday, average Joe. She'd thought that was funny. The more she got to know Joe, the less she thought about Zorro. The spark that night was nothing compared to the blazing fire that sprang up between her and Joe.

Studying him now, she knew nothing would ever put out that fire. Not the Lewis women's family curse. Not other people. Not time and old age. In five days, Joe's dad, Pastor Owen Clarke, would say the words, "What God has joined together, let no man separate." And that would be that.

For now, she needed to stop worrying that something would happen between today and Wednesday.

Joe caught her eye and nodded. She nodded back. Time to go. Tonight was the last night they would have alone together before they got married. Between the wedding and Christmas, it had been a busy month, and it would only get busier.

They said their goodbyes, Joe quickly accepted the rest of the cookies, and they made their way out to Joe's truck.

"They seem nice," Joe said. "Too bad you won't be working there again after the honeymoon."

"Yeah," Tori agreed, "I'd love to work for Faith. I hope her business grows enough that she can bring on permanent employees soon. Maybe I'll still be temping and she'll call me."

Tori smiled as Joe opened the truck door for her and handed her in. Such a gentleman.

"Are you sure you don't mind me temping for a while?" she asked when he climbed in the driver side. "I know I should probably get a real job, but I haven't found anything that makes me say, *this* is what I've been waiting my whole life to do. You know? I'm good with people. I'm a fast learner with tech stuff. But I haven't found a good mix yet. Maybe I should get a job at the Apple store," she joked.

Joe squeezed her hand as he pulled onto the street. "We'll manage," he said, "whatever you decide to do."

Tori smiled at Joe's profile. Good man, through and through. She sighed. She was so lucky. So *blessed*.

Joe took her left hand and kissed her ring finger near her

engagement ring. He held her hand while he made a turn, then he said with a grin, "You're staring."

Tori giggled. "Where are we going? This isn't the way home." They only lived a few blocks away from each other, so they obviously weren't going to either place right now.

Tomorrow, Joe's friends were going to move her belongings into Joe's house, and she'd stay with Lexie starting tomorrow night. The whole "moving into his house" concept still seemed surreal. She wondered how long it would take before she'd be comfortable saying "our" house.

"It's our last night alone for a few days, so I thought we should enjoy it."

"Um, you remember we have stuff we have to do tonight, right?"

"We still have to eat." He nibbled on one of her fingers until she giggled.

"Yes, yes, all right." Tori pulled at her hand. "Focus on your driving, mister."

Joe drove another ten minutes and pulled into the parking lot of a steakhouse Tori knew he loved. Actually, she wasn't sure if a steakhouse existed that he wouldn't love. Barely half-full at this hour, the restaurant provided quick service and hot, delicious food.

When Joe was nearly done with his steak, he cut another bite and paused. "You know I couldn't love you any less than I do right now. You know that, right?"

Tori put down her fork and lay her hand on his. "I feel the same way. It's crazy how much I love you," she said, feeling her throat tighten. "I can't imagine my life without you now."

Joe appeared to consider her words.

"Are you worried..." Tori felt a spike of anxiety lance her heart. "Do you think we shouldn't..."

It took a moment for Joe to follow her unspoken question. "No!" His startled expression underscored the truth of his denial, and Tori relaxed.

"You still want to, right?" he asked. He put down his fork and squeezed her hand.

"Oh, yes!" Tori chuckled in relief.

"Okay, good. No, I was just thinking…I wanted you to know that even though we haven't known each other very long, there's nothing you could do or say to make me love you less." He looked a little worried again. "Whatever we may learn about each other in the future."

Tori tried to figure out what was going on in his head. Was there something he wanted to tell her? Something he was afraid she'd find out? Something…oh no, something he'd found out about her?

She tried not to pull away. He loved her. She knew it. He'd just said it again, promised his feelings wouldn't change. "Has someone said something?" she asked, trying to focus on breathing evenly. "Told you something about me?"

"Oh, honey, no," Joe's expression changed again, back to his protective look. "There is nothing anyone could say that would change how I feel. I was just thinking that we haven't known each other very long, and…things are bound to come up that may surprise the other, and…" He shrugged. "I'm sure it will all be fine."

Ah, she got it now. He was afraid she wouldn't like something she might find out about him. She tried to lighten the mood. "You mean like if I found out you like country music?"

He made a face. "That is never going to happen. Metallica all the way, baby."

He'd said things before about not liking country. Tori pushed his buttons. "Or if you found out I like country music?"

"Don't even joke about that."

"Would you still love me if you found out I own some Garth Brooks CDs? It's great road trip music. You'll love it."

"That's not funny." Joe put one hand on his chest. "You're killing me."

She giggled. "Rascal Flats, too."

"Stop, just stop." Joe's comical expression morphed into laughter and he kissed her knuckles before letting go of her hand and picking up his fork.

"You're not an ax murderer," she said with a smile. "You haven't bilked thousands of people out of their retirement money, right? I can't imagine finding out anything bad about you."

She meant it, too. Joe was the epitome of Mr. Nice Guy.

"Maybe you'll learn more about my job, wish I were in a different line of work." His voice sounded casual.

Tori tried to soothe his concerns, whatever they were. "You work in security, keeping people safe," she said. "What's not to like about that? I'm proud of you, Joe. You walk your talk. I haven't met a lot of people who can do that. You're my hero." She gave him a flirtatious look.

Joe smiled and took her hand again, pulling it against his cheek. "Like a superhero?"

"No, a *real* hero. Not a Saturday morning cartoon. You really help people when they need it. That's a wonderful thing. I'd like to find a job like that."

Until recently, Tori had worked with the single-minded goal of making enough money to help take care of her nephew. Temp jobs with few benefits paid more than the full-time jobs she'd looked into, and she could take time off if Ben was sick. But now that Lexie was on her feet, Tori could start thinking about what she wanted to do with her life, not what she had to do.

"Come on," Joe said in a teasing voice, "wouldn't you like to meet a real superhero?"

"Like Batman?" Tori laughed. "If I ran into Batman in our neighborhood, he'd scare the crap out of me! Really, if you'd never seen any of the movies to know he was a good guy, you'd take one look at him and assume it was all over. Pearly gates, here I come."

Joe chuckled and shook his head. "Maybe. But I think if you met a real superhero you'd know you were safe."

"You're the one who makes me feel safe," Tori said, pulling his hand to her lips and kissing it.

Joe looked like he was going to say something else, but the waiter interrupted to ask if they had room for dessert. Tori thought about the flourless chocolate cake she'd seen on the menu, but Joe told the waiter they'd pass.

"Eat too many cookies earlier?" she teased.

Joe raised his eyebrows a couple times. "You'll see. You want a to-go box?"

With the rest of her meal wrapped up, they put on their coats and gloves and hats and scarves. Even without much snow, the temperatures had dipped into the 20s every night not long after the sun went down.

Joe pulled her close as they walked to the truck. She loved his physical nature. His easy manner helped her to relax and allow herself to be a bit more demonstrative, in public and in private. She normally only let her guard down when she hung out with her siblings, especially with her little brother, Kevin. She'd spent so much energy over the years trying to please her mother, and staying away from men because they might ruin her life, she'd sort of lost herself. Hanging around Joe's excessively huggy family reminded her that she rather liked physical displays of affection.

She sighed happily.

Again Joe drove in a direction not toward home. He made a couple of turns into a residential neighborhood and hit the buttons to roll down the windows partway. What was he doing now?

Tori started to ask when she heard the Christmas music. She gasped in delight as Joe turned right and pulled into a long line of cars driving very slowly through the brightly lit street.

"Christmas lights?" She clapped her gloved hands. "That's one of my favorite parts of Christmas!"

ALSO BY KITTY BUCHOLTZ

CONSIDER BUYING BOOKS DIRECT FROM
KITTY! GO TO KITTYBUCHOLTZ.COM / BOOKS

Adventures of Lewis and Clarke

Superhero in Disguise

A Very Merry Superhero Wedding

Unexpected Superhero

My Bullheaded Superhero Valentine

Also...

Adventures of Lewis and Clarke: The Beginning (the first three
books)

The Strays of Loon Lake

Welcome to Loon Lake

Love at the Fluff and Fold

Traverse City in Love

Cherry on Top (free short story)

Little Miss Lovesick

Death and Tacos (coming soon!)

A NOTE FROM KITTY

I hope you enjoyed reading *Superhero in Disguise*. This story always makes me smile! I originally wrote it as the beginning to *Unexpected Superhero* in the Adventures of Lewis and Clarke series. But introducing the two main characters on the day they met made the book feel like a romance, and I wanted more action. So I pulled the scene.

One day, it suddenly hit me what I'd been saying with this piece: we're all trying to find out who we are and who we were meant to be, and we'll discover along the way that there are forces at work around us to help and hinder our quest.

Once I figured that out (consciously, my subconscious already knew!), the edits to the newly titled *Superhero in Disguise* were made in just a few days. Exciting times for a writer!

If you liked this story, you'll also want to read *A Very Merry Superhero Wedding*, Tori and Joe's Christmas Eve wedding during a Christmastime crime spree, and *Unexpected Superhero*, when Tori finds out why she's different. (You can read all three stories in the omnibus, *Adventures of Lewis and Clarke: The Beginning*.) Then their best friends, Bull and Hayley, finally go out on a real date in *My Bullheaded Superhero Valentine*.

My books are available as ebooks and in print at most online retailers. *Unexpected Superhero* and *Little Miss Lovesick* are also available as audiobooks. All the ebooks, print books, and audiobooks will be added to my own web store over the course of 2024. Purchases there support me and my work in a significantly greater way so I'd love it if you'd like to buy from me directly (kittybucholtz.com/books)!

You can also join my free or paid membership community over on Patreon (links at the end of About the Author). Read chapters early before the books even come out, discuss the stories with other readers, see fun art about the settings of the books, and more!

You might also try my romantic comedies in the Traverse City in Love series and the Strays of Loon Lake series. You can read *Cherry on Top* for free. It's set in the same town as *Little Miss Lovesick* during the famous National Cherry Festival. It's my gift to you when you join my reader newsletter at kittybucholtz.com/freebook. Enjoy!

If you really want to make my day, I'd love for you to post your thoughts about the book in a review. Thanks so much!

And just so you know, I rebranded all my books in 2024 to be "sweet" — so no swear words or overt sex scenes. I hope you enjoy the change.

Happy Reading!

ABOUT THE AUTHOR

Kitty Bucholtz writes sweet romantic comedy and superhero urban fantasy, often with an inspirational element woven in. Her stories feature women whose sense of humor and nervous gutsiness get them into and out of all kinds of trouble. She grew up forty miles east of Traverse City, Michigan—a town that is a smaller but surprisingly similar version of Double Bay, Michigan, the setting of this book. She went to college there, met and married the love of her life, and waved goodbye to everything she knew when she and her husband, John, struck out for parts unknown.

Their romantic adventures have included a scolding at Parliament House in Belfast for canoodling, three trips Down Under where her handsome hubby made animated movie animals look real, and a delicious taste of European life living in Sweden. After earning her M.A. in Creative Writing in Sydney, she formed Daydreamer Entertainment and began self-publishing. Founder of Write Now! Workshop and Write Now! Workshop Podcast, she loves to teach and coach writers.

Only God knows where they'll wind up next – but they're pretty sure it will be another cool chapter in their adventure!

If you enjoyed this or any of Kitty's books, please leave a review—they are a tremendous help to both writers and readers!

Connect with Kitty today!
kittybucholtz.com/
kitty@kittybucholtz.com

Get your copy of the free short story *Cherry on Top* at kittybucholtz.com/freebook today!

patreon.com/kittybucholtz

tiktok.com/@kitty_bucholtz

facebook.com/kittybucholtzauthor

bookbub.com/profile/kitty-bucholtz

amazon.com/author/kittybucholtz

x.com/KittyBucholtz

instagram.com/kittybucholtz

goodreads.com/kittybucholtz

youtube.com/kittybucholtz

www.ingramcontent.com/pod-product-compliance
Lightning Source LLC
Chambersburg PA
CBHW020605130626
46552CB00007B/3046